Snow-White and Rose-Red

A Grimm's fairy tale
illustrated by
Gabriele Gernhard Eichenauer

Floris Books

A poor widow lived in a secluded little cottage. In front of the cottage there was a garden with two rose-bushes standing in it. One had white roses and the other had red roses. The widow had two children who were just like the rose-bushes. One was called Snow-White and the other Rose-Red. They were as good and devout, hard-working and cheerful as any two children in the world ever were, but Snow-White was quieter and more gentle than Rose-Red. Rose-Red loved to run about in the meadows and fields, looking for flowers and catching butterflies, but Snow-White would sit at home with her mother, helping her with the house-work, or reading aloud to her when there was no work to be done.

The two children loved each other so much that they always went hand in hand whenever they went out. Whenever Snow-White said: "We shall never leave each other," Rose-Red would answer: "Not as long as we live," and their mother would add: "Whatever the one has, she should share with the other."

Often they
would walk about in
the woods alone gathering
red berries, but no animal ever did them
harm but came quite trustingly up to them. The little hare
would eat a cabbage leaf out of their hands, the roe grazed
beside them, the hart bounded joyfully past them while the
birds stayed on their branches singing for all they were worth.
No accident ever befell them. If they stayed late in the woods
and night overtook them they would lie side by side on the
moss and sleep till morning came, and their mother knew
and was not anxious about them.

Once when they had spent the night in the wood and the dawn had woken them, they saw a lovely child in a shining white garment sitting near where they lay. The child stood up and looked at them in a friendly way, but said nothing and went away into the wood. When they looked round they saw that they had been sleeping near a precipice and would certainly have fallen over the edge if they had gone a few steps further in the darkness. Their mother told them that it must have been the angel that watches over good children.

Snow-White and Rose-Red kept their mother's cottage so clean and tidy that it was a joy to look into it. In summer, Rose-Red looked after the house and every morning she brought a bunch of flowers for her mother and put them by her bed before she woke up, and in the bunch was a rose from each bush. In winter Snow-White lit the fire and hung the kettle on the hook. The kettle was made of brass, but it shone like gold, so well had it been scoured and polished.

In the evenings, when the snow-flakes were falling the mother would say, "Snow-White, go and bar the door." Then they sat by the hearth, and their mother took her spectacles and read aloud from a big book, while the two girls listened as they sat and span. Beside them a lamb lay on the floor, and behind them on a perch sat a little white dove with its head under its wing.

One evening as they were sitting thus cosily together, someone knocked at the door as if he wanted to come in. The mother spoke: "Quick Rose-Red, go and open the door, it must be a wayfarer seeking shelter."

Rose-Red went and drew back the bolt thinking it would be some poor man, but it was not; it was a bear who thrust his thick black head in through the doorway. Rose-Red cried out and sprang back, the little lamb bleated, the little dove fluttered up into the air and Snow-White hid behind her mother's bed. The bear, however, started to speak and said: "Do not be afraid, I will do you no harm, I am half-frozen and I only wish to warm myself a little in your house."

"You poor bear," said the mother, "lie down by the fire, only be careful not to singe your fur."

Then she called, "Snow-White, Rose-Red come out, the bear will not hurt you, he is to be trusted."

Then they both came forward, and bit by bit the lamb and the dove drew near and lost their fear of him. The bear spoke: "Children, beat the snow a little out of my fur."

Then they fetched a broom and swept the fur clean while he stretched out by the fire and, much at ease, growled contentedly. Soon they became quite familiar and began to play mischievously with their clumsy guest. They tugged at his fur with their hands, put their little feet on his back and rocked him back and forth, or they took a hazel-rod and beat him, and when he growled they laughed. But the bear did not mind at all, only when they overdid it, he would cry:

"Leave me alive, children,
Snow-White, Rose-Red
You'll strike your wooer dead."

When it was time to go to sleep and the others had gone to bed the mother said to the bear: "In God's name you may stay and lie by the hearth and you will be sheltered from the cold and the bad weather."

As soon as the grey dawn came, the two children let him out and he trundled off over the snow into the woods. From now on the bear came every evening at the same time, lay down by the hearth and allowed the children to play with him as much as they wished; and they were now so used to his coming that they did not bolt the door until their black companion had come in.

When spring came and outside all was green the bear said one morning to Snow-White: "Now I must go away and cannot come back all summer."

"Where are you going, dear bear?" asked Snow-White.

"I must go into the wood and guard my treasures from the wicked dwarfs. In winter when the ground is frozen hard they have to remain below and cannot work their way up and out, but now when the sun has thawed and warmed the earth, they break through and climb out. Then they search and steal: whatever comes into their hands and lies in their hollows cannot easily be brought back into the daylight."

Snow-White was quite sad at the parting. When she drew back the bolt of the door for him and the bear pushed his way out, his fur caught on the latch of the door and a piece of his hide was torn off. Snow-White thought that she had seen gold shining through, but she was not quite sure. The bear hurried away and soon disappeared among the trees.

After a time the mother sent the children into the wood to gather firewood. There they found a large tree that lay felled on the ground, and by the trunk something was jumping up and down in the grass, but they could not make out what it was.

When they came nearer, they saw it was a dwarf with a wrinkled old face and a snow-white beard an ell long. The end of the beard was caught fast in a cleft of the tree, and the little man was jumping like a dog on a leash, not knowing what to do. He stared at the girls with his fiery red eyes and screamed: "What are you standing there for? Can't you come and help me?"

"What has happened to you little manikin?" asked Rose-Red.

"Silly nosy goose," answered the dwarf, "I wanted to split the tree, to have small pieces of wood for the kitchen fire. With thick logs the little food that our kind needs is easily burnt, for we don't guzzle as much as you coarse greedy folk. I had already hammered in the wedge properly, and all would have gone well, but the cursed wooden wedge was too smooth and it flew out unexpectedly, and the tree snapped together so quickly that I was not able to pull out my lovely white beard. Now it is stuck in the tree and I can't get away. And you silly, smooth milk-faces are laughing. Bah, how repulsive you are!"

The children tried hard, but they could not pull the beard out, it was jammed in too tight.

"I'll go and get some people," said Rose-Red.

"You mutton-headed chumps," screeched the dwarf, "what do you want to fetch more people for, you're two too many already, can't you think of anything better?"

"Don't be impatient," said Snow-White, "I will soon get you out."

She took her scissors out of her pocket and cut off the end of the beard. As soon as the dwarf felt he was freed, he seized a sack full of gold hidden between the roots of the tree. He pulled it out muttering to himself: "Uncivilized rabble, cutting off a piece of my good beard, a pox on you!"

Then he slung his sack on his back, and off he went without even looking at the children.

Some time after this, Snow-White and Rose-Red wanted to catch some fish for supper. When they came near the stream, they saw something like a big grasshopper hopping towards the water as if it were going to jump in. They ran up and recognized the dwarf.

"Where are you going?" asked Rose-Red. "You surely don't want to jump into the water?"

"I'm not such a fool," cried the dwarf. "Can't you see the cursed fish is trying to pull me in?"

The little man had been sitting there fishing and unfortunately the wind had entangled his beard in the fishing-line. When a big fish had taken the bite the weak creature had lacked the strength to pull the fish out. The fish had the upper hand and was pulling the dwarf after it; and although he clutched at stalks and rushes, that did not help him much, for he had to follow the movements of the fish and was in imminent danger of being pulled into the water. The girls had come in the nick of time: they held him fast and tried to release the beard from the line, but in vain, beard and line were hopelessly entwined.

There was nothing for it but to take out the scissors and cut off the beard, and a little bit was lost. When the dwarf saw that, he screamed at them: "Do you think that's civil, you toads, to ruin a person's face? Wasn't it enough to spoil the end of my beard, without cutting off the best part of it? I shan't be able to show myself to my own people. Buzz off, and run till your feet fall off!"

Then he fetched his sack of pearls which was lying in the reeds, and, without saying another word, he lugged it away and disappeared behind a stone.

It so happened that soon afterwards the mother sent the two girls off to the town to buy thread, needles, tape and ribbons. The way took them over a heath where huge boulders lay strewn here and there. They saw a great bird hovering in the air and slowly circling over them. Then it sank lower and lower until it finally alighted not far from one of the rocks. Immediately afterwards they heard a piercing cry of pain. They ran towards the sound and saw with alarm that the eagle had seized hold of their old acquaintance the dwarf, and was about to carry him off. The compassionate children held tightly on to the little man and struggled with the eagle for a long time until he let go of his prey. When the dwarf had recovered from his first fright he cried in his raucous voice: "Couldn't you have treated me a bit more carefully, you've let my thin coat get so torn that it is all shreds and holes, you awkward, clumsy clots!"

Then he took a sack of jewels and crept under the rocks into his hole. The girls were already used to his ungratefulness, went on their way and did their shopping in the town. When they came again to the heath on their way home they took the dwarf by surprise as he was emptying out his sack of jewels on a clear space, for he did not think that anyone would be coming by so late.

The evening sun was shining on the sparkling stones, and they were glittering and gleaming so gloriously in all colours that the children stopped to look at them.

"What are you standing there gaping for?" screamed the dwarf, and his ashen grey face became scarlet with rage.

He was going to go on scolding, but a loud growling was heard and a black bear came trundling out of the wood. The dwarf jumped up in a fright but he could not reach is hidey-hole as the bear was quite close. He cried out in terror: "Dear bear, spare me, I will give you all my treasures. See my beautiful jewels lying here. Grant me my life. I'm such a scraggy little wight I wouldn't do you any good. You would hardly feel me between your teeth: look, take hold of those two godless girls, they would be a tender morsel for you, they're as juicy as young quails, eat them up for heaven's sake!"

The bear took no notice of his words, gave the evil creature one single blow with his paw, and he never moved again.

The girls had run away, but the bear called after them: "Snow-White and Rose-Red, do not be afraid, wait I will come along with you."

Then they recognized his voice and stayed where they were, and when the bear was beside them suddenly his bearskin fell from him, and he stood there as a handsome man, all dressed in gold.

"I am a king's son," he said, "and was bewitched by the godless dwarf who had stolen my treasure and condemned me to roam the woods as a wild bear until I should be released by his death. Now he has got his well-deserved punishment."

Snow-White was married to him and Rose-Red to his brother, and they shared with one another the great treasures which the dwarf had gathered in his hollow. The old mother lived for many years peacefully and happily with her children. She took the two rose-bushes with her, and they stood in front of her window and every year bore the loveliest roses, white and red.

Translated by Donald Maclean

First published in German under the title *Schneeweisschen und Rosenrot*
© 1986 Verlag Urachhaus, Johannes M. Mayer GmbH, Stuttgart
This translation   ©   Floris Books, 21 Napier Road, Edinburgh 1986

British Library CIP data available

ISBN 0-86315-044-6   Printed in West Germany